D1230457

WITHDRAWN

Mom's Busy Days

For my princess and my cupcake—ER

For Christel, my perfect friend—EM

Published by
MAGINATION PRESS ®
750 First Street NE
Washington, DC 20002

Magination Press is a registered trademark of the
American Psychological Association.

For more information about our books, including a complete
catalog, please write to us, call 1-800-374-2721, or visit our website
at www.apa.org/pubs/magination.

English translation by Jenna Miley
Book design by Susan K. White
Printed by Worzalla, Stevens Point, WI

Library of Congress Cataloging-in-Publication Data
Names: Raucy, Elise, author. | Meens, Estelle, illustrator.
Title: Mom's busy days / by Elise Raucy ; illustrated by Estelle Meens.
Other titles: Folles journees de Maman. English
Description: Washington, DC : Magination Press, [2018] |
Audience: Age: 4-8.
Identifiers: LCCN 2017024576| ISBN 9781433828201 (hardcover) |
ISBN 1433828200 (hardcover)
Subjects: LCSH: Mother and child–Juvenile literature. |
Parenting–Juvenile literature.
Classification: LCC HQ755.85 R38313 2018 | DDC 306.874/3–dc23 LC
record available at https://lccn.loc.gov/2017024576

Manufactured in the United States of America
10 9 8 7 6 5 4 3 2 1

Mom's Busy Days

by Elise Raucy
illustrated by Estelle Meens

MAGINATION PRESS • WASHINGTON, DC
American Psychological Association

My mom *is* really busy!

"Come on, Maggie, hurry up! Here, take your skirt and tights."

"Ethan, come here, stop clowning around.
Take the trash out later sweetheart
so you can finish your coffee."

Mom has a lot to do everyday.

"Come on, let's go. We have to drop Dad off at the train station,
drive Maggie to school, take Ethan to the babysitter,
and I have to buy some bread for dinner!"

Mom can do a thousand things at the same time.
"Yes, hello? No, I'm alright, Francine. Hold on two seconds.
Maggie, put your feet on the floor.
Ethan, play with something else."

"I'll call you back later, Francine . . . "

"Bye honey,
have a good day…"

"Kids, wave
bye-bye to Dad!"

Mom is sometimes late.
"Oh, no! We're late. Hurry up,
I just heard the bell ring and
Ms. Jennifer is already inside!"

And sometimes Mom must work late, too.
"Honey, can you try putting your puzzle together
on your own? I can help you soon."

"I still have some more work to do, little man.
About 20 more minutes.
Hold on a little longer and play with your car.
Mom isn't done yet."

Sometimes Mom has too much to do.

"Eeek! There are crayon marks on the table.
Maggie? Ethan? What happened?"

"No, I'm not laughing!"

But sometimes, Mom says time flies by too fast.

"Five years old already! You're getting so tall pumpkin…"

"And who is this big boy?
Oh! My little man is growing
up so quickly."

So Mom finds the time to be just with us.

"What fun things are we going to do today? Play hide-and-seek?
Dance a silly dance? Sing at the top of our lungs?
And what if we had . . . a tickle fight!"

"Look at this beautiful cake we made.
Nothing but delicious ingredients—butter, flour, and sugar.
One, two, three, four eggs. And what else? Chocolate! Yummy!"

We forget about schedules, carpools, and busy time.
"Look Ethan, that cloud looks like a horse.
Or a sheep with a funny head.
What do you see Maggie?"

We find time to play.

"Here Maggie, catch.
Now pass it to your brother.
Well done!
Can you throw the ball to Mom, honey?"

"Go ahead, sprinkle the seeds, Maggie. Very good.
Now you, Ethan, water them well…
Soon we'll have some pretty sunflowers!"

We cherish time together.
"Look at how beautiful the trees are, Ethan.
Oh! The dog found a pretty leaf…
Pick it up Maggie, we'll put it in your scrapbook."

"Come snuggle in close to me, sweethearts.
Big hug! Rest your head on my shoulder, pumpkin.
Come here in my arms, honey."

Sometimes Mom stops time. . .

. . . and it feels like it will last forever!

Note to Parents and Caregivers
by Julia Martin Burch, PhD

Parenting is beautiful, rewarding, exciting, and HARD WORK. As Maggie describes in *Mom's Busy Days*, "My mom is really busy! Mom has a lot to do everyday. Mom can do a thousand things at the same time." Sound familiar? Research suggests that parents today are busier than ever, balancing caring for their children with work outside of the home, chores, appointments, and extracurricular activities, among many other responsibilities. Yet, in the midst of the busy, fast-paced, and joyful life you and your family lead, you are likely also acutely aware of how quickly your children are growing up and how fast the little moments slip away. It can be overwhelming to simultaneously stay on top of your many responsibilities and take care of yourself and your children, but there are tools that can help you make the most of and savor these special years with your children!

Create mindful moments.

As depicted in *Mom's Busy Days*, life in many families today is incredibly busy. Parents wear many hats, shifting from mom, to coworker, to chef, chauffer, and homework helper– sometimes all in a matter of minutes! It can feel very challenging to find quality time to spend with your children on a daily basis, but mindfulness is a great tool to find balance in a packed schedule. Mindfulness has become a popular buzzword and has taken on many different meanings; however, at its core, being mindful simply means paying attention to the present moment, both inside and outside of yourself, without judgment. This means noticing with all five senses what is going on around you and letting any internal thoughts, feelings, or urges simply be present without

concentrating on them or evaluating them. Being mindful does not have to entail a daily meditation practice. In fact, just giving yourself permission to not do five things at once and instead, to simply tune in and intentionally pay attention to moments with your child for a minute or two every day is a mindfulness practice. You'll be amazed at what you notice and how you can create small moments of clarity and calm in your busy day by simply tuning in and being totally present.

For example, in those maddening morning moments, when it feels as though every family member is going in a different direction and everyone has an incredibly pressing need right *now*, you can still practice mindfulness. Notice any emotions rising in yourself. Frustration? Anxiety? Perhaps even enjoying the chaos of your happy home? We often try to push emotions away in moments of stress; however, research suggests that by noticing and labeling our feelings ("I'm starting to feel overwhelmed"), our emotion in that moment actually subsides. Once you've mindfully noticed and labeled your emotions, take a deep breath and move forward with the morning.

You can also practice mindfulness by focusing completely on the activity at hand—fully throwing yourself in and participating. For example, when you and your child play with clay together, pay attention to the colors, textures, smell, and temperature of the clay. Ask your child what she notices using all five of her senses. Help her cultivate a spirit of openness and curiosity by doing the same in yourself. You can also practice mindfulness by leaving your self-consciousness at the door and fully immersing yourself into whatever activity your child has in mind like the tickle fight in *Mom's Busy Days*. Have that wild kitchen dance party. Sing loudly with her while you walk through the park. Being fully present in the moment allows us to savor the little things while reducing stress.

Create rituals.

Rituals are a part of every culture. They help us feel connected and like we are part of a group or community larger than ourselves. Family rituals give children a sense of stability and connection and offer a predictable routine amidst the daily hustle and bustle. You might have many rituals from your family of origin, or you may be creating completely new rituals with the family you have made. Whichever is true for you, involve your children in your family rituals. Explain where they came from and tell stories of your own experience of rituals as a child. These experiences and stories become part of a child's developing self-identity.

Rituals do not always have to be large affairs, such as holiday celebrations or birthday parties. You and your children can create small, daily rituals, such as doing a bedtime routine in a similar order each night, having the same special breakfast treat every Saturday morning, or going to a particular park on Sunday afternoons, among many other options. One easy ritual to establish is having each member of the family answer the same "check in" questions at dinner each night or before bedtime. For example, each family member could share their favorite part of the day or something fun or interesting that happened to them. As children get older, you can each share a "rose" (highlight of your day), a "thorn" (low point of your day), and a "bud" (something you are excited about for tomorrow).

A consistent family meal is also an excellent way to create stability and connectedness in an on-the-go, hectic family environment. Research has found that families who consistently (around four times per week) eat a meal together tend to have more physically, emotionally, and psychologically healthy children. For some families, dinner is a convenient time to gather, but for others it might be breakfast. Adapt the ritual to your family's needs and have fun creating a special space which you can all look forward to each day amid your busy schedules.

Model healthy coping.

Life overwhelms every parent at times. This never feels good and can feel particularly bad when the resulting frustration and anger boils over at your children, as when Maggie and Ethan draw on the table. The good news is that hidden within these difficult moments are unparalleled opportunities to show your children healthy ways to cope with stress and strong emotions. You can label your feelings for your child ("I am feeling sad and mad") and reassure him that he is still loved ("but I still love you very much"). You can then talk through how you are going to cope with these feelings ("I need to take a little break and go for a walk," or "I am going to take some deep breaths to help my body calm down"). Children learn by watching you and this approach normalizes strong emotions for children and teaches them appropriate ways to calm themselves down. That being said— no one is perfect! So in those moments that you find yourself coping in a less helpful way, such as yelling or storming off, you can always speak calmly to your children afterwards and explain what you were thinking and feeling and how you would like to act differently the next time you are upset.

Finally, one of the best things you can do as a busy parent is to take care of yourself. This is often a hard sell for parents who cannot imagine more finding time in the day, but self-care does not always have to be a time-consuming undertaking. In any given day, taking care of yourself might simply look like tapping into your mindfulness skills and truly paying attention to and enjoying your morning cup of coffee. Maybe self-care is going for a short walk once the children are in bed or watching a funny show with your partner (without multitasking!). It's up to you to find moments to care for yourself in your day-to-day schedule, so figure out what works best for you and your family. Don't be afraid to call in the reinforcements—grandparents, babysitters, friends, or your community—to give you a little time to yourself. Ensure that you regularly create time in your busy schedule to see friends or keep up with hobbies you enjoy. If stress persists, is overwhelming, or interferes with everyday life, it might be helpful to consult a psychologist or other mental health professional. The old adage "it takes a village to raise a child" remains true, so please be gentle with yourself and respect your own limits. It is not easy, but as you practice self-care parenting will become more satisfying and fulfilling in the long run.

JULIA MARTIN BURCH, PhD, is a postdoctoral fellow in child and adolescent psychology at McLean Hospital. Dr. Martin Burch completed her training at Fairleigh Dickinson University and Massachusetts General Hospital/Harvard Medical School. She works with children, teens, and parents, and specializes in cognitive behavioral therapy for anxiety, obsessive compulsive, and related disorders.

About the Author

ELISE RAUCY was born in February 1978 in Medan, Indonesia. Adopted at the age of two months, she lived a happy childhood and joyful adolescence in Virton, Belgium. She developed a love of reading as a child and borrowed hundreds of books from the local library, devouring everything that she could get her hands on. She later discovered her love of writing. From poems to songs, short stories to writing competitions, she is passionate about playing with words. She is also a translator.

About the Illustrator

ESTELLE MEENS was born on August 11th, 1976 in Hermalle-sous-Argenteau, Belgium. She studied illustration at the Saint Luc Institute in Liège. She has published several children's books and has been working as a painter since 2006.

About Magination Press

MAGINATION PRESS is an imprint of the American Psychological Association, the largest scientific and professional organization representing psychologists in the United States and the largest association of psychologists worldwide.